Trini's
Big Leap

Alexander de Wit & Beth Kephart
illustrated by William Sulit

penny
candy
BOOKS

Penny Candy Books
Oklahoma City & Savannah

Text © 2019 Alexander de Wit & Beth Kephart
Illustrations © 2019 William Sulit

 This book is printed on paper certified to the environmental and social standards of the Forest Stewardship Council™ (FSC®).

Acknowledgments: The authors and illustrator wish to thank Randy McCoy, Senior Executive of Product Leadership for The Little Gym International, who shared a story that sparked Trini's tale. We thank as well Alexis Orgera and Chad Reynolds of Penny Candy Books, two rare poet-publishers whose mission is to create books that matter and who have engaged with us, from the very start, in an inspired and happy collaboration. We wish also to thank Shanna Compton for her gorgeous packaging of Trini's tale—the bounce of the text, the bright blue of the mood. Finally, we would not have made this beautiful connection without the care, dedication, and sheer goodness of our agent, Karen Grencik.

Photo of Alexander de Wit: Nathalie Gabay
Photos of Beth Kephart & William Sulit: William Sulit
Design: Shanna Compton

23 22 21 20 19   1 2 3 4 5
ISBN-13: 978-0-9996584-5-1 (hardcover)

Small press. Big conversations.
www.pennycandybooks.com

Trini could do anything.
It was a little embarrassing, to be honest.

She was the highest flyer, the strongest gripper,
the most spectacular cartwheeler at Bounce and Build.

She was ridiculously good. A regular aeronaut.
A stellar acrobat. An Olympic hopeful.

"I can do that," Trini always said.
"I can do that."

And, all by herself, she did. Trini was always ready.

It was so much fun being terrific.

"What did you do today?"
Trini's mother would always ask.

"Everything!"
Trini would answer.

"Everything?" her mother would ask.

"Everything's so easy."

And then one day, after all her leaps
and twirls and swirls and curls...

Trini stopped to look around.

There they were—Freddie and William,
Juniper and Keisha—with the most amazing
start of things at their very fingertips.

"I can do that," Trini said, and hurried in.

Trini began at once. She thought of all the majestic things that she might make. A house? Too small. A museum? Too common. A castle?

Yes, of course. That was it.
A castle with a tower!

"I can do that!" Trini said.

Too long.

Too short.

Too crooked.

Too wobbly.

This was not a castle
with a tower.

"Would you like some help?" Mr. Ed asked.
"No," Trini said. "I can do it."

"I *can't* do it."

"Maybe," Freddie said, "we can do it together."

"Trini!" her mother called, when Trini
could not be found at her usual pickup spot.

The next day, at the exercise mats,

Trini was ready.

"You can do that,"
Trini told Freddie.

"You can do that,"
Trini told Juniper.

"You can do that,"
Trini told Keisha.

And in their own
ways, with Trini's
help, they did.

"You want to build a taller tower?" Trini asked
Freddie and William, Juniper and Keisha.

"yes," they said.

"We can do that."

Afterword

Trini flies in the world of gymnastics. She likes to run, jump, do a forward roll. It is easy for her, and she feels that there is nothing she can't achieve. When children spontaneously engage in activities they enjoy and quickly assimilate, their confidence tends to rise.

Children are also faced with activities and skills that are challenging to them but not necessarily to others of the same age. These are key moments in their development.

Trini discovers that building a castle with her hands is not, for her, so easy. She wonders why. She is, at first, confused and frustrated.

So, should she just focus on what she is good at and not lose time and maybe confidence doing an activity that does not come naturally?

Exposing children to a variety of experiences stimulates their development as well as their ability to deal with the diverse tasks and situations they will face as they grow up. Soon Trini will need to do things with her hands, deal with challenges, and overcome obstacles through collaboration with her peers.

Why does it matter, now?

Still, why expose children to challenging tasks when they are young, when it seems they have their whole lives to learn? Here's one reason. Each of us is born with most of the neurons we will ever have. While connections between neurons that have been stimulated get reinforced, others fade away as children grow up. The consequence is that learning is most natural and spontaneous in our early childhood. Early childhood is, in fact, that time when we establish the foundations for our future development.

Hence the benefit of offering our children a diverse set of experiences and stimulations. For instance, learning to confidently design and hand-build things is not just relevant to those children who will be naturally attracted to creative and manual jobs when they grow up but to all of us as we engage in the many daily tasks that rely on hand skills—from cooking or healing a wound to drawing an idea or persuading an audience. It is also, and more fundamentally, an opportunity to develop life skills that will serve us throughout our lives, such as learning to learn, persevering, and working with a team.

Here's another important reason not to give up on a more challenging task: Taking such a thing on exposes a child to an activity that may turn out to become a true passion—and a life calling. When we gain the confidence to use our hands to express our ideas and creativity, then initial talent can become secondary. The passionate, confident child has a better chance at becoming what she hopes to become, no matter what "natural" gifts she was born with.

Watch for the perception you create

Neuroscience reveals that, when a child can behave according to her preferences, she will feel more fulfilled and happier, independent of the outcomes. The purpose of exposing a child to a variety of activities should therefore not be to try and convert the child to activities that we feel *should* become passions. The purpose should be to help her build strong enough foundations so that she will be able to navigate life without experiencing fear, anxiety, frustration, anger, or loss of confidence when she has to walk outside of her comfort zone.

The choices we make as parents and other adults in these scenarios will inevitably shape the ways our children grow and the people they become. They will influence whether the "homey" child will happily develop the ability to operate and feel comfortable in social settings, even if it will always require a level of effort and will never be her natural preference—or whether social settings become a recurring source of stress that result in feelings of agitation, tension, discouragement, or helplessness.

The key is in the how

When Trini fails to build a castle by herself, she is at first discouraged. Remember, she refused Mr. Ed's help at first because she's used to doing things on her own. What happens next matters. For example, if someone comes and builds the castle for her, this "help" will likely reinforce her feeling of being incapable. She may also be tempted to flee and go back to the gym. Instead, she accepts her friends' offer to work together. By joining forces with them, Trini feels accomplished for two reasons: she has succeeded in her goal of building a castle and she has learned that people working together can move mountains.

Conversely, if Trini feels part of a nurturing learning environment, where it is not about *being* the best, just *trying* her best, she will give *her* best and enjoy the experience. Trini's story teaches the importance of creating a safe context for children so that they can embrace new, positive learning experiences, and reminds us as well of what parents might do as they support their child's journey. Our children don't just listen to the words we use; they "listen" to our behaviors, and if we're comfortable with new experiences, it shows.

Trini may or may not discover a new passion as she builds that castle with her friends. That is not the point. The point is that Trini will have tried something new and reinforced her confidence in herself, in her abilities to take on a challenge, and in the power of working as a team. She will be able to build on that experience next time she faces a new situation, with new tools. She will have learned to go from an idea in her head to concrete execution with her hands. She will have learned perseverance. Finally, she will have learned to play a different role in a team and to welcome help. All of which will serve her well during her entire life. Next time Trini is faced with a challenge, she'll hear, deep within herself, those positive words: "Yes, you can do it." Or maybe even: "We can do it."

Way to go, Trini!

Alexander de Wit
Founder and CEO of The Little Gym Europe
Board member XSEED Education

Alexander de Wit is an entrepreneur, investor, and advisor. A Dutch national, he lives in Belgium and works out of Brussels, London, New York, and Singapore. Alexander has founded many successful companies, including The Little Gym Europe, a market leader in child development programs with franchises in Europe and the Middle East. His passion, and the common denominator to his many pursuits and activities, is to help people develop their potential. Married and the father of three children, Alexander enjoys discovering the world with his family, practicing alpine skiing and waterskiing, and acrobatic trapeze. *Trini's Big Leap* is his first picture book.

Beth Kephart is the award-winning author of more than two dozen books, a teacher of writing at the University of Pennsylvania, and a cofounder of Juncture Workshops. Her essays, reviews, and interviews appear in publications ranging from the *New York Times*, *Life Magazine*, *Chicago Tribune*, and *Washington Post* to *Ninth Letter*, *North American Review*, *Catapult*, *Literary Hub*, *Salon*, and *Brevity*. Beth never mastered the perfect cartwheel, though she tried for a very long time. She was much better at the Hula-Hoop, and she loved to skate, both on wheels and on blades. She used to ballroom dance, but now she dances when no one is looking. Most of the time she writes books for all kinds of readers about characters she admires and would hope, someday, to meet. More can be found at bethkephartbooks.com.

William Sulit is an award-winning illustrator, ceramicist, and designer. Born in El Salvador, he studied design at North Carolina State University and received his Masters of Architecture degree from Yale University. After working as an architect, graphic designer, and photographer he has turned his attention to ceramics and illustration as his primary means of artistic expression. He is the cofounder of Juncture Workshops and he collaborates with his wife, Beth Kephart, in life, business, and art.